SANDMARE

For Cory and Addy

SANDMARE
A YOUNG CORGI BOOK: 0 552 547174

PRINTING HISTORY
Young Corgi edition published 2001

1 3 5 7 9 10 8 6 4 2

Set in 16/20pt Bembo Schoolbook by Falcon Oast Graphic Art Ltd

Young Corgi Books are published by Transworld Publishers,
61–63 Uxbridge Road, London W5 5SA,
a division of The Random House Group Ltd,
in Australia by Random House Australia (Pty) Ltd,
20 Alfred Street, Milsons Point, Sydney, NSW 2061, Australia,
in New Zealand by Random House New Zealand Ltd,
18 Poland Road, Glenfield, Auckland 10, New Zealand
and in South Africa by Random House (Pty) Ltd,
Endulini, 5a Jubilee Road, Parktown 2193, South Africa

Printed and bound in Great Britain by
Cox & Wyman Ltd, Reading, Berkshire

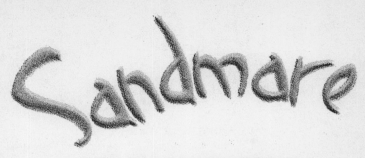

Sandmare

HELEN COOPER

ILLUSTRATED BY TED DEWAN

YOUNG CORGI

UNIVERSITY OF CHICHESTER

CONTENTS

Chapter One
THE SAND HORSE

"Draw a horse," called Polly.

Dad pulled a face. Horses are hard to draw.

"Please," Polly begged. And the sand was just right for drawing on.

Dad reached for a piece of shell.

He used it to draw
some sharp, pointy lines
like these. They were the
ears.

Next he drew a
gentle curved line
towards the nose. Then
the line flicked around
the mouth, curved
up under the chin,
and glided down to
make the horse's neck.

"I need an eye," he
shouted.

Polly was ready. She
held out a round
brown pebble.

"Perfect." Dad
smiled. He looked hard
at the drawing. Then
he popped the pebble
right where the eye
should be.

Now the horse was alive. Drawings often come to life once the eyes are in the right place. They can't usually move. But sometimes they can think. This horse could. And it knew that it was a special drawing, even when it was only halfway done.

"That back leg's wrong," said Polly.

"I know," sighed Dad. "I can't do legs."

In the end he let Polly cover most of the back leg with a thick swishy tail. They couldn't hide the front legs so he only drew one. It didn't look too bad. And the horse didn't mind. It was happy with two legs.

Polly drew in a mane with her finger.
"Is it a she horse?"

"A mare?" said Dad. "Could be."

"Yes, I am a mare," whispered the
horse so quietly that no-one heard.

"I think she's fantastic," breathed
Polly. "It's sad that the waves will wash
her away when the tide comes in."

Dad took some chicken out of the
picnic basket.

"When will the waves come in?"
munched Polly.

"Just after sun-
set," said Dad,
holding out the
wishbone.

"So I have the rest of the afternoon," whispered the Sandmare to herself. Well that's not so bad . . . But I wish I wasn't trapped in the sand.

SNAP went the wishbone.

Polly waved the long end. "I wish that the Sandmare could run free."

They peered down at the Sandmare. Dad rubbed Polly's hair.

"That sort of wish doesn't often come true," he smiled.

Not often maybe! But Polly and the Sandmare had wished at the same time, so the wish was very strong.

Chapter Two
THE WISH

The picnic was packed away and Polly had put on her shoes. She leaned over and whispered, "Good luck," into the Sandmare's ear.

Then she was gone.

"There's still the wish," murmured the Sandmare hopefully. She was sure she could feel it quivering and crackling around her. But it had better work soon. Those waves are coming nearer.

The sun had noticed the wish as it toasted the beach with its oven breath. Now that the beach was empty, it called down to the sea, "I think we have to give that horse drawing a chance."

"Why bother?" the sea sighed. "I've swallowed whole centuries of sand drawings. That one will be mine in the end, just like the rest."

"And yet," whispered the beach drowsily, "there will still be sand left, after you've swallowed it up. The Sandmare is my child."

"The Sandmare wants to escape from both of you," reminded the sun.

"Where could it escape to?" moaned the sea. "There is nowhere safe for a creature like that."

"Perhaps if it ran very far . . ."
murmured the beach.

"Very far," agreed the sun. "There is
some hope . . . but only if the Sandmare
tries her hardest, and doesn't give up."

The sea was bored. "I'll give the
creature one night to try," it hissed.

The beach shrugged beneath the
Sandmare. "One night then," it rumbled.
"She'll be back to sand in the morning."

"I bet she doesn't even leave the
beach," gurgled the sea.

I'll show them, thought the
Sandmare. She struggled to shake herself
free. Nothing happened. She was still
stuck fast. What shall I do? She stared
up at the sun, hoping for help. None
came. The sun had slipped behind a cloud.

A scruffy long-nosed dog, out for its evening walk, pattered along the beach.

It stopped to snuffle around the Sandmare. If you have ever been flat on your back with a wet dog snuffling around you (a dog you have never met), then you will know how the Sandmare felt. She had to stare up at the dog's muddy tummy. She had to feel the dog's damp, sniffling nose, and smell the doggy breath. Then the dog lifted up its back leg and . . .

"DON'T!" screamed the Sandmare.

The dog leapt sideways. "I beg your pardon," it barked. "I was just . . . um . . ."

"Well do it somewhere else," snorted the Sandmare.

The dog disappeared behind a rock. Then it came back wagging its tail. "You talked," it woofed. "You hummfed, and you shouted, and your nose moved. Do it again."

The Sandmare twitched her nostrils.

"See!" yapped the dog, jumping up and down. "See."

The Sandmare found she could frown. "There was a wish," she said. "I think it must be working a bit."

"Is a bit enough?" panted the dog. "Can you get up now? Those waves are pretty close."

The Sandmare peeped at the sea from the corner of her pebble eye. The waves had almost reached her tail yet she still couldn't budge.

The dog trotted around her. "Try harder."

Sandmare strained as hard as she could. Her muscles shook, her tail swished . . . But that was all.

"I'll wish too." The dog squeezed its eyes shut.

And now the Sandmare found that she could lift her head . . . But what was the use of that without the rest of her?

The effort was making her tremble all over. The beach seemed to throb around the part of her still in the sand.

"Come *on*," woofed the dog. "The water's almost touching you."

"I'm trying so hard that it's making me shake," neighed the Sandmare.

The dog pricked up its ears. "You're not shaking!" it barked in alarm. "That's the beach ponies. They gallop this way at sunset. You've got to move!"

The Sandmare could hear the thudding too.

"They won't see you," panted the dog. "Quick! You'll be trampled."

"Now or never!" The Sandmare struggled frantically.

She could hear the ponies blowing on the sand.

She could see the next wave splashing towards her, the wave that would wash away her tail.

And at that second, a last spindle

spike of orange sunlight winked through
the clouds and touched her hooves.
Up she bounded in a shower of sand,
shaking her mane, and whisking her tail
from the water.

Chapter Three
THE BEACH PONIES

You can imagine how wonderful it was
for the Sandmare when she ran for the
first time. All that cool sunset air woosh-
ing through her mane, while the ground
sped away beneath her hooves.

"Catch the stars!" whinnied the
beach ponies as the evening star
appeared in the sky.

"Yes! Catch the stars," answered the
Sandmare, straining ahead. She joined

the beach ponies in their wild gallop and felt that she could race for ever.

Of course, she didn't gallop like the flesh and blood ponies. Don't forget she only had two legs. She had to find her own way of moving. Sometimes she rocked from one leg to the other, front, to back, to front again, like a rocking horse. Sometimes she moved her two legs in, then out, then in again, like a pair of scissors. Best of all she bounced on both legs at once like a spring lamb. But not too high. There was a man riding one of the ponies way behind them. He hadn't seen the Sandmare so far, and she wanted it to stay that way.

Now the man called out to the ponies, "Steady there." To the Sandmare's confusion, the ponies slowed to a trot and went through a gate, into a scruffy field.

Luckily the man must have wanted his supper. He shut the gate and walked away without noticing the Sandmare. The Sandmare held her breath until he had gone.

Then she burst out, "We didn't catch the stars."

The ponies all turned round and stared at the Sandmare. The lead pony was called Anchor because of the shape of the splodge on his tummy. "It's just a game," he snorted. "We never really catch the stars. They're too far away."

"But I need to go somewhere far away," said the Sandmare. "If I'm still here in the morning I'll turn back into sand."

The beach ponies sucked air through

their teeth. "You won't get very far in one night," explained Anchor. "You're not very fast, you know."

"I have to try," whinnied the Sandmare.

"How far do you need to go?" neighed a grey pony called Silver.

The Sandmare was flustered now. "I don't know, just far . . . maybe as far as the stars."

"You can't possibly," snorted Silver. "The church clock just struck six. There's only eleven hours before morning."

The other ponies stamped their feet and looked embarrassed. Then an old black pony called Velvet lifted her head from the scrubby grass. "Isn't there someone else who might help you?" she asked.

"There was a girl," said the Sandmare. "She was nice. She drew my tail."

"Then she must be quite clever," nodded Velvet. "Why don't you ask her?"

"There you go," neighed Anchor. "She made you. She should know what to do."

"But you've got to find her first," warned Silver.

"The golden horses might know where she is," whinnied a young black pony.

"They're meant to be very wise," agreed Velvet.

"Look to the end of the beach," said Anchor. "Do you see the Shining City stretching out onto the  water? You'll find them there, in a beautiful round temple."

"But you mustn't look them in the eye," said Velvet. "Always look down. It's bad to look them in the eye."

"Why?" asked the Sandmare.

There was silence for a moment.

"We don't know. We've never seen them," said Anchor. "But when we were foals we were always told . . ."

"It's polite," hurumphed Velvet. "It's the right way to talk to them. Just wait until the people have gone home. Then see what the golden horses have to say."

 "And be careful," warned Anchor. "They may not be quite safe."

Chapter Four

THE MERRY-GO-ROUND HORSES

More stars twinkled as the Sandmare dashed along the beach. They don't look that far away, she thought. I bet I

could reach them right now. Those ponies gave up far too easily.

So she tried. She rocked, and she scissored, and she bounced across the beach, and stretched upwards until she was exhausted. But the stars seemed as far away as ever. And she was even more disappointed when she looked over at the "Shining City". She could see now that the lights only shone from a seaside pier. The kind with dodgems, and a striped helter-skelter, and scruffy pink-and-blue booths selling candy floss

and chips. There was no sign of a
golden temple. Gloomily she
rested in the shadows
of the steps and won-
dered what to do
next.

Then she spot-
ted the splendid
merry-go-round
with its glittering
horses. "Maybe
that's what the
beach ponies
meant," she
whispered.
Now she
could hardly wait
for the people on the
pier to go home. But
they didn't for ages. It was
nine o'clock when the music
stopped, and children finished
swinging on the plastic gorilla.

Half past nine when the lights went out, leaving only one dim red bulb flashing atop the helter-skelter. The Sandmare crept forward and red shadows shimmered in the mirrors of the merry-go-round. "No need to be scared," she told herself. "It's only that spooky red light." She gave a little bow towards the red and gold horses, and carefully looking away from their eyes, she blurted out, "Excuse me . . ."

"We know why you came," sang an eerie wooden voice.

A whole chorus of others joined in,

all chanting together, "We know you. We know everyone on our beach."

The Sandmare shuffled her feet. It's hard not to look up when you're waiting for someone to speak. She glanced sideways at them. Which one had spoken first? The one with the jewelled crown?

"C-Could you tell me where to find the girl who helped to make me?" she stammered. (She only looked up as far as its spangled neck.)

"The child can't help you." (It was the one with the crown who spoke.)

Then the whole ghostly horse choir joined in, chanting, "You belong to the beach and the sea. Go back where you belong, Sandmare." And slowly, as if blown by the wind, the merry-go-round began to circle.

"Please," called the Sandmare. "The little girl might be able to help me escape from here."

"Why would you want to leave?" they sang.

"Come closer," called the crowned horse. "Look at the sea."

The Sandmare crept forward. There was a good view from the pier.

"Can you see them?" hummed the crowned horse. "Can you see the white horses dancing on the waves?"

"I can see froth," frowned the Sandmare.

"Froth?" he said gravely. "Do you think you are the only sand horse we have seen?"

"There have been many," the horse choir joined in.

"All those white horses were once drawings too," droned the crowned horse. "Go back to the beach, Sandmare. Let the waves take you. You should be with the other white horses of the sea."

"Must I?" the Sandmare wondered. The merry-go-round spun faster now. It made her feel dizzy.

Suddenly a rich voice boomed out from behind the merry-go-round.

 "Sorry to interrupt. But if you ask me, 'white horse' is just a fancy name for foam on the waves."

The Sandmare tried to see who had spoken. "I don't want to be foam," she whinnied.

"Quiet," commanded the crowned horse. It was a soft, steady sort of command but very firm. The Sandmare forgot the advice of the beach ponies. She looked up into the face of the crowned horse. Red light twizzled in his secret painted eyes. Immediately the Sandmare felt heavy, and weary, and confused.

The church clock struck ten.

Look away, she thought.
She couldn't.

"Go back to the sea," lulled the whirling horse choir.

Look away, she told herself again.

35

It grew colder. A night wind rattled the shutters of the burger booths, swung the strings of light bulbs, and clanked the pleasure boats against the pier.

Eleven o'clock struck . . . Then twelve . . . Still the Sandmare gazed on in a trance.

"Maybe I should go back to the sea," she murmured.

The rich mystery voice spoke urgently. "Sandmare, are you still there? You shouldn't be listening to those wooden heads. They don't know as much as they make out. It's time you spoke to someone else."

"I wanted to speak to that little girl," exploded the Sandmare.

"Children know nothing," sniggered the horses gently through their painted teeth.

"I'd still like to find Polly . . ." muttered the Sandmare.

"Polly! Why didn't you say so. I see her all the time," called the mystery voice. "Come on now. You're strong. Get out of there while you still can."

"Go to the sea," sang the horses.

But the Sandmare had woken up. "Not until I have to," she decided. She closed her eyes tight, shut off her ears, and sprung sideways and away, before they could call her back.

Chapter Five
THE GLASS HORSE

"Thank goodness," said the voice.

The Sandmare opened her eyes. She was standing in front of the plastic gorilla.

"Ask *me* about Polly," he boomed. "I know all about her. She never bothers with that bunch of wooden idiots. One of 'em threw her off when she was little. I looked after her. Now she comes and pats me every day . . . after she's visited the glass horse."

"Where can I find her then?" asked the Sandmare.

The gorilla scratched his ear. "Find her? Oh I don't know where you could find her . . . But she'll be here this afternoon.

Just wait here with me."

The Sandmare felt like crying.
"I can't wait," she whinnied. "Haven't
you any idea where she lives?"

The gorilla pulled at his eyebrow.
"The glass horse might know. Polly talks
about him. He's in a shop. Go straight
across the road, and it's on your left. You
could ask him."

The Sandmare thanked the gorilla.
"I'll go there right now," she neighed.

The shop was cluttered with hats and
biscuit tins, tangled together with a
dressmaker's dummy, two bird cages, a
stuffed fox and a jar full of peacock
feathers. The glass horse was wedged
between a mermaid jug, and a mug
with the queen's head on it. He was half
rearing, and he had a broken stump on
his shoulders.

"Excuse me," said the Sandmare, nosing the window. "Could you tell me where to find Polly?"

The glass horse narrowed his eyes. "Little Polly you mean? Freckles? Curly top? Big teeth?"

The Sandmare nodded eagerly.

"Why do you want to find her?" asked the glass horse.

"I hope she'll be able to help

me," said the Sandmare. And she told the glass horse about the wish. The church clock struck one as she finished.

The glass horse nodded thoughtfully. "So you have to run. Where were you thinking of running to?"

"That's the trouble," frowned the Sandmare. "I only know that it has to be far away. I . . . I did think of going as far as the stars but now I know that was silly. There isn't enough time for that."

"Hey, you run after your dreams," encouraged the glass horse. "Go for it. You might not get there, but you might not end up on the beach either."

"But how will I get up there?" whinnied the Sandmare.

The glass horse sighed. "Probably have to fly. And wings aren't easy to come by." He peered ruefully at his

broken shoulder. "I should know. Used
to have wings myself."

"Goodness, I'm so sorry," murmured
the Sandmare.

"Never mind me." The glass horse
perked up. "You're a drawing. All you
need is someone to draw you some
wings."

"Polly drew my tail," said the
Sandmare.

"Then she should be able to manage
wings," brayed the glass horse. "She's a
clever girl."

"Do you know where she lives?" shuffled the Sandmare.

"I did," pondered the glass horse, waving his foot. "Now let me think. Polly's mother bought a rocking horse from here. A mean moody old thing. Hope you don't run into him. Anyway, he kept boasting about where he was going. The Blacksmith's Inn. That was the name of the place. I think Polly must live there."

The Sandmare gave an excited whinny. "The Blacksmith's Inn? That definitely sounds like Polly's house."

"I'd head uphill if I were you," said the glass horse. "I've watched her go that way."

"Thank you so much," said the Sandmare.

"You're welcome," the glass horse called after her. "Just don't listen to *anyone* telling you to give up . . . And watch out for that rocking horse. His mood swings when he does. He can turn quite nasty."

Chapter Six

THE ROCKING HORSE

"His mood swings when he does? What could the glass horse have meant by that?" the Sandmare wondered aloud. Still it gave her something to think about as she dragged herself up the steep hill. Her legs seemed weaker than they used to be. They ached terribly. She didn't make it to the top of the hill until two o'clock. But she was in luck. The Blacksmith's Inn was right there.

No door was open of course. "But all

the windows
are shut too,"
puzzled the
Sandmare.
"How will I get in?"
Then she spotted
a tiny door
set within the front door. It was really
meant for a cat. "Maybe if I make
myself really
small . . ."

She curled up
tight, in the way
you might roll a
ball of paper. Then
she launched her
ball-self at the cat-
flap. It swung open far too easily.

"Too fast," she gasped as
she bowled across the hall.
She stuck tight under
some curved
wooden struts.

46

"Now where am I?" She partly unfurled to look. Then she curled up like a hedgehog. She had rolled straight under the rockers of the rocking horse.

"I see you," called a creaky voice. "Come out."

There was no point in hiding. She peeked her eyes and nose out. The rock-ing horse was facing straight ahead so he seemed to look down his black spotted nose at her.

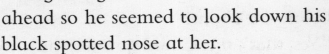

"Hello there," he smiled pleasantly. "Now what can you be doing under my rocker?"

"I . . . I came to find Polly," croaked the Sandmare uncurling a little more.

In uncurling she pressed against the
rocker, and tipped the rocking horse
back a teeny bit.

"Have I got this right?" murmured
the rocking horse. "Could you possibly
be the sand drawing that Polly's been
babbling on about?"

"Yes, that's me. Could you tell me
where she is?" the Sandmare asked,
uncurling further against the front
rocker.

The rocking horse swung back even
more. "I certainly will not tell you

where she is," hissed the rocking horse, glaring at the ceiling. "Hasn't she done enough for you already?" He sounded so angry.

"I didn't think Polly would mind," the Sandmare said, unrolling completely to try to explain.

The rocking horse tipped almost over. "Mind?" he snarled. "I mind. I'm the house horse. I decide who sees Polly. AND I'VE DECIDED TO CRUSH YOU!"

Desperately the Sandmare strained to escape but in her struggle she accidentally kicked the hall rug under the rocking horse's back rocker. Down swung the front rocker, pinning her onto her back.

"Now he will do it," the Sandmare shuddered. "I shall be crushed sand in Polly's hallway."

The crunch didn't come. The rocker rested gently on her back.

"Let's be sensible." The rocking horse gazed down at her mildly. (He was tipped forward now.) "You can't see Polly in the middle of the night without a good reason."

The Sandmare trembled. She understood what the glass horse had meant now. He only gets nasty when he swings backwards, she thought. But how will I escape without tipping him again?

"So?" asked the rocking horse. "Why do you want to see Polly?"

"I . . . want her to draw me some wings," gabbled the Sandmare. "I need them so I can fly to the stars, and I have to fly there before sunrise."

"Oh dear. You want to fly to the stars?" crooned the rocking horse. "You don't really believe in that do you? And you seem so tired now. Yes, I think you may be beginning to crumble. It is almost morning."

"Maybe he's right," worried the Sandmare, as the church clock struck three. There did seem to be rather a lot of sand around her feet. But she thought of the glass horse. "I mustn't give up," she told herself. She kicked the rug out from the back rocker, and flung herself away from the front one.

The rocking horse swung wildly.

CLONK!

"I'll squish you!" he snarled, his teeth snapping at the ceiling.

CLUNK!

"Be sensible old thing," he creaked, tipping forward again.

CLONK!

Somehow she'd spun towards his back hooves. They were kicking towards her.

"Up here," piped a tiny voice.

The Sandmare leaped for the stairs.
There was a roar behind her. The
rocking horse banged its back hooves
on the floor.

"Forget him," called the tiny voice.
"Come up to the top,
quick."

Chapter Seven

THE TOY HORSE

The Sandmare scissored up two flights of stairs. A fierce little pony on wheels was waiting for her, a yellow pony with blue spots, a proud puffed chest and a bristle mane.

"I'm Biddle," he announced, whirring his wheels on the spot. "Hurry up. Come on in."

He bustled the Sandmare through a green door and at last . . . there was Polly, kneeling up in bed, bouncing from side to side with excitement. The Sandmare felt so relieved and happy that she couldn't even speak, but that didn't matter. Polly had plenty to say.

"You took a long time," she said. "But we had a feeling you'd come so Biddle watched for you. You're quite safe now. We'll look after you. You can live in the wardrobe and . . ."

The Sandmare found her voice. "I can't," she neighed. Miserably she told Polly how little time was left, and how she needed wings, and how it was probably all too late anyway.

She looked very disappointed but she nodded bravely. Polly sat back on her heels and listened.

"Never mind. Don't you worry. We'll sort you out somehow. Only . . . I'm not sure how to draw your wings. You're not lying on the sand anymore."

"I know where you can draw," smirked Biddle. "Help me move the bed." He pushed his forehead against the bedpost. Polly scrambled to look.

"Oh, I see." She smiled. "Clever Biddle."

When the bed was in the middle of the room, Polly made the Sandmare lie down on the floor where the bed had been. The Sandmare didn't much want to. That bit of floor was thick with dust and fluff, and she could feel a sticky toffee paper prickling her tummy. She soon stopped minding. Polly was drawing wings in the dust above her shoulders.

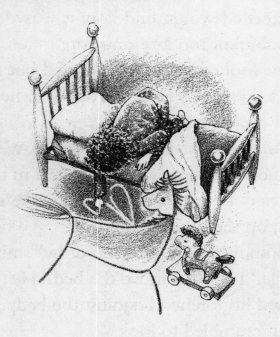

"That's good drawing," nodded Biddle.

The Sandmare craned round to look too. "Are they joined onto me?" she asked.

Polly smoothed the dust lines into the sand ones. "They are now." She wiped her hands. "Try standing up."

The Sandmare stood and the dust wings came too.

"Yey," cheered Biddle, revving his wheels.

"But I can hardly feel them," worried the Sandmare. "They aren't made of the same stuff as the rest of me. They don't seem very strong."

"They'll work just fine," said Polly, opening the window and sniffing the air. "But it's almost morning. You'd better get going."

"You're not allowed out there, Polly," warned Biddle.

"I'll watch from here," Polly said, helping the Sandmare through the window.

The Sandmare stumbled out onto the roof. She tried not to notice the sand that was billowing from her legs as she wob-bled there.

"Go on," bossed Polly, looking at the sky. "It's time to go. I'll wish on a star for you." She picked out the brightest star, pointed at it, and screwed her eyes shut. "There. It's done," she said. "Time to fly."

The Sandmare twitched her shoulders. The dust wings hardly moved. They didn't feel part of her at all. "But I've got this far," she told herself. "I can't give up now just because I feel tired." She planted her wobbly feet as firmly as she could, screwed up her eyes and expected to fly.

"Try harder," encouraged Polly when nothing happened.

The Sandmare's ears drooped. "It's not working."

"Of course it is," frowned Polly. "I wished, didn't I? It worked yesterday."

"It did," nodded the Sandmare more bravely. She tried again.

After a bit, Biddle said, "Maybe the Sandmare is like an aeroplane. Maybe she needs a runway."

They all looked along the gentle slope of the roof.

"And I think," said Polly quietly, "for a good take-off she'll need wheels."

"But I don't have wheels," said the Sandmare.

"Biddle does."

Chapter Eight

SANDMARE ON WHEELS

"No!" piped Biddle. "She's not having my wheels!"

"But you could give her a ride," pleaded Polly.

"She's too big!"

"Not on your back," explained Polly. "Look at your wheel platform. There's enough room for the Sandmare to put one hoof in front of you and one hoof behind you. Then when you're going really fast she'll take off."

"But I won't be able to see where I'm going," squawked Biddle furiously. "And how will I get home afterwards?"

"I'll come and find you," said Polly.

"You're not allowed out on your own."

"No-one'll know. I'll be very quick . . . Please, Biddle." Polly stroked Biddle's bristles. He liked being stroked. "It'll be all right," Polly pleaded.

The Sandmare wasn't so sure. There wasn't much room for her feet on that wheel platform. "It might not be safe," she mumbled.

"Are you saying my wheels aren't safe?" bawled Biddle.

"No," the Sandmare protested. "But what if I don't fly? You'll get hurt if we crash."

"My wheels never crash," roared Biddle.

It was half past four in the morning.

"Go on," wheedled Polly. "Wheel down the roof with Biddle, and flap your wings. When you're going fast enough . . . you'll take off."

The Sandmare looked up at the stars. They were fading fast. It was almost dawn.

"Don't you think my wheels are good enough?" said Biddle, huffily hopping down to the tiles. He swivelled his wheels to keep himself from rolling.

"OK," the Sandmare decided. "I'll do it."

"Get on with it then," said Biddle, wriggling.

Polly said, "Jump on and push with your back leg."

The Sandmare hobbled and hopped . . . and pushed and . . .

"Wheeeeee . . ." she whinnied as they zoomed along the roof.

"Hold your wings out to catch the wind," called Polly.

The Sandmare did. It was thrilling. Almost at the edge of the roof now, she stared ahead, ready to lift off . . . when she caught sight of the first flush of dawn. "I'm too late!" she wailed and that was when everything went wrong.

Pandemonium!

The wind drove into her, side on as if she were a sail, and the wheel platform whooshed sideways. There was nothing Biddle could do. They were out of control.

BANG! They jolted off the roof.

BUMP! They landed on top of the bay window.

Sand crumbled from the Sandmare, hitting Biddle full in the face.

"Fly, you dust-ball," he squealed as they plunged BASH! WALLOP! onto the kitchen extension.

They were still rolling but the Sandmare shook with despair. "I can't do it. It's no use . . ."

"Don't give up now, Sandmare," shouted Polly. "It's not too late. The sun isn't up yet."

But the Sandmare didn't hear. She was panicking too much to listen.

THUMP! They smacked into the sand pit.

RUMBLE! They hared down the path . . .

"You've got to steer away from the hill, Biddle," yelled Polly.

"I can't see where I'm steering," howled Biddle. "There's sand in my eyes. Why did you let this lunatic near my wheels?"

Polly shouted louder. "Come on, Sandmare . . . You could still take off."

"Just flap, grit-head!" bawled Biddle. "Or we'll smash to pieces."

Once again the wind slammed into the Sandmare. They careered down the hill.

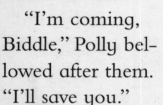

"I'm coming, Biddle," Polly bellowed after them. "I'll save you."

"She'll be too late," panicked Sandmare as they hurtled towards the pier.

"Can't you jump off or something?" snarled Biddle. "We'll hit the merry-go-round any minute."

"I'll stop somehow," gasped the Sandmare. But she was too nervous to try flying, and as more sand scattered away from her she found that she couldn't even move her weak legs now.

"Yuck! Can't you control that sand stuff?" spat Biddle.

THUD! They hit the wooden boards of the pier.

"Got to save Biddle," said the Sandmare frantically. "Got to do something."

The merry-go-round loomed above them when she desperately threw her whole body sideways.

"Whoooaaa!" Biddle screamed. The wheel platform swerved, and they slammed to one side. They just missed the merry-go-round. "Now we're going to fall off the end of the pier," shouted

Biddle. "And I don't think I'll float."

"HELP, SOMEBODY!" screeched the Sandmare.

Somebody heard. Out whisked a giant arm. Up in a gorilla hug went Biddle.

But a gust of wind blasted the

Sandmare out from the gorilla's grasp.
She was light as litter now that
so much sand had crumbled away.
She tumbled along the pier, past the
candy-floss stands, and the burger
booths, onwards to the end of the pier.

"Slipped out of my hands," groaned
the gorilla. "She won't stop in time.
She'll be in the sea any minute. She's
had it."

"Wait,"
said Biddle.
"Look!"

Chapter Nine
THE FLYING HORSE

The Sandmare was blown into the
mouth of the helter-skelter. There must
have been wind in the tunnel too. Up
she skidded, rocketing up the slippery
chute. Just as suddenly, the tunnel ended.
She shot outdoors, still on the chute.
More fresh air now, and a good view if
she wanted to look. The Sandmare
didn't want to look. "What happens
when I reach the top?" she whinnied.
"What happens then?"

She couldn't feel the wind behind her
anymore, couldn't work out why she
still spiralled upwards. There was an odd
swishing sound just behind her ears.
From the corner of her eye she caught

sight of something moving. She turned
to look.

Her wings were flapping, carrying
her up the chute.

She was spinning round the last spiral
now. Skimming the railings, shooting up,
and up, her wings twisting like
helicopter propellers. And she was light
enough now for the dust wings to lift
her into the sky. Flying at last. But even

as she rejoiced,
the first red
rays of the sun
crept over the
hills. For a
moment she
glowed and
twinkled in
the light, then
the last of her
lines scattered
into sand and
dust.

"Too late,"
sighed the
Sandmare.
"It's morning.
Time to fall back to the sea."

But a dawn wind bundled the sand
and dust upwards. Of course, the pebble
eye was too heavy. It dropped below.
Without it the Sandmare couldn't see
anymore.

"But I can still think," she realized, as the whirlwind of sand rose into the sky. When the warm wind rolled higher it cooled. Tiny drops of water coated all her dust and sand grains. And soon they were part of a fluffy, clingy mist.

The Sandmare didn't know that a cloud is made when teeny fragments of water and dust drift together in the sky. But what was left of her began to understand something, as she floated over the land and up towards the brightness. "I'm still chasing a star!" she realized. And she spoke the truth. For the sun is the nearest star of all.

Polly reached the pier out of breath, just as PER-CLATTER, a brown pebble fell from the sky, bounced once, and rolled to her feet. Polly picked it up. She had held it before.

"It's the Sandmare's
eye," she whispered.

"So the wings didn't work,"
croaked Biddle.

But the gorilla wasn't so sure.
"It might be something she didn't need
anymore," he said.

A pink cloud, like a piece of pulled
candy floss, drifted over the sun. Polly
had seen that sort of cloud before.
She knew the name of it.

"A mare's tail cloud." She smiled.

This is how the long, drawn out, strokes of cloud looked.

"That cloud looks awfully familiar," Biddle said. "Just like one of your drawings."

"I think so too," grinned Polly, rolling the pebble in her hand.

THE END

ABOUT THE AUTHOR

HELEN COOPER is a full-time illustrator and writer of children's books. Her childhood was spent in Cumbria, but she now lives in London with her husband, Ted Dewan and young daughter. As well as being a highly talented artist, Helen is also a keen musician who studied music at college and worked as a music teacher before turning to writing and illustrating full time.

Helen has not had any formal art college training but taught herself with the help of books from her local library. Her first book, *Kit and the Magic Kite*, was quickly bought by Hamish Hamilton and published in 1987, with Corgi publishing the paperback in 1989.

Since then she has illustrated over fourteen books and her work has been translated into fifteen languages. Her titles for Transworld now include *The Bear Under the Stairs, Little Monster Did It!, The Baby Who Wouldn't Go to Bed* which won the 1996 Kate Greenaway Medal and *Pumpkin Soup* which was shortlisted for the 1998 Kurt Maschler Award and also won the 1998 Kate Greenaway Medal.

Helen is the first ever author/illustrator to have won the Kate Greenaway Medal with two consecutive books.

Visit Helen Cooper's website at www.WormWorks.com

ABOUT THE ILLUSTRATOR

TED DEWAN has been an illustrator and cartoonist since 1988. His work regularly appears in the *Daily Telegraph, Sunday Times, The Times Educational Supplement* and the *Guardian*. He won the coveted Mother Goose Award for his first children's picture book, *Inside the Whale*, in 1992. Subsequent picture books include *The Three Billy Goats Gruff* and *Top Secret*. He has also illustrated children's and adult non-fiction. His first book for the Doubleday list was *The Sorcerer's Apprentice*, which was shortlisted for the Kurt Maschler Award. He lives in London with his wife, artist and Kate Greenaway Medal-winner, Helen Cooper, and their young daughter.

Crispin, the Pig Who Had it All was commended for the Kate Greenaway Medal, 2000 — one of the most prestigious awards for children's illustration. The judging panel said of the book: "The bold, exuberant illustrations catch the reader's eye first, and then closer examination shows just how every page is crammed with extraordinary detail... This story contrasts the emptiness of materialism with the warmth of friendship as it follows Crispin's heartwarming journey to understanding."

Visit Ted Dewan's website at www.WormWorks.com

The Shrimp

Emily Smith

Wild life!

Ben spends the holidays with his nose in
the sand and bottom in the air. It's not
because he's shy – though some of his
classmates do call him the Shrimp. It's
because he's got a great idea for his
wildlife project.

A competition is on! The class projects
are going to be judged by a famous
TV wildlife presenter, and the prize is
irresistible. Ben would love to win it, but
others have their eyes on the prize too…

An exciting new story from
an award-winning author.

Young Corgi books are perfect for
building reading confidence.

ISBN 0 552 54735